JUN 2019

Willow Moon Publishing

Lancaster, Pennsylvania

Marcy Mabel Mollie McMann

Written by Alison T Broderick

Illustrated by Mina Anguelova

Willow Moon Publishing
108 Saint Thomas Road, Lancaster, PA 17601
willow-moon-publishing.com

Cataloging Data
Broderick, Alison T, Marcy Mabel Mollie McMann/ by Alison T Broderick; illustrations by Mina Anguelova
Summary: Marcy Mabel Mollie McMann learns the importance of washing her hands after she gets sick.
Hardcover ISBN: 978-1-948256-15-5 {1. Juvenile Fiction. 2. Girl Fiction 3. Health & Wellness Fiction 4. Stories in rhyme}

This book is dedicated to my husband, Matt - my strength, my supporter, my soulmate.

Marcy Mabel Mollie McMann
Never bothered to wash her hands.

2

A rough-and-tough girl at the age of eight,
She played outdoors from morning 'til late.

3

She'd splash in the rain during summer bike rides,
Collect slimy bugs for gooey mud pies.

4

Stomp in puddles and cross through creeks,
Take cover in caves during hide-and-seek.

5

She loved climbing trees and taking catnaps,
Getting sticky like glue from the maple tree sap.

She'd play in the dirt and dig for worms
Head home for dinner, covered in germs.

Big Sister complained to Dad and Mom,
"Marcy smells bad, like a stinky stink-bomb!

8

With hands on her hips, Mom lowered her eyes,
She shook her head slowly and then replied,

"To the bathroom you go, Miss Marcy Mae.
Clean up the mess from your adventures today."

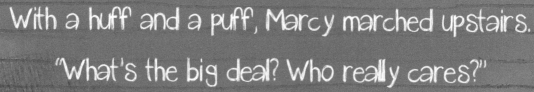

With a huff and a puff, Marcy marched upstairs.
"What's the big deal? Who really cares?"

12

She agreed to give her hands a quick scrub
'Cause all she wanted was to gobble some grub.

13

The problem with messy Marcy McMann

Is she never used soap when washing her hands.

14

Although she rinsed the dirt down the drain,

Without a good lather, the germs would remain.

15

The very next morning when she awoke
Dad made Marcy scrambled eggs and toast.

Instead of her usual cheerful face,
Marcy was sneezing all over the place!

17

Her head was pounding, her throat was sore.

She coughed and sneezed, then coughed some more.

19

Dad put his hand on the front of her head,
"You have a high fever. Go right back to bed."

20

No outdoor fun for Miss Marcy today.

No mud pies, long bike rides, or pool-time play.

21

Sad and discouraged, she took Dad's advice.
Her head on the pillow felt really nice.

22

"Come into the office," the nurse declared.
They hopped in the van and drove straight there.

24

A check of the ears and a look down her throat,
A listen to her heart using his stethoscope,

25

The doctor told Marcy she would be OK
As long as she rested for the next few days.

26

"You must always remember, Marcy McMann,
It's very important to wash your hands."

27

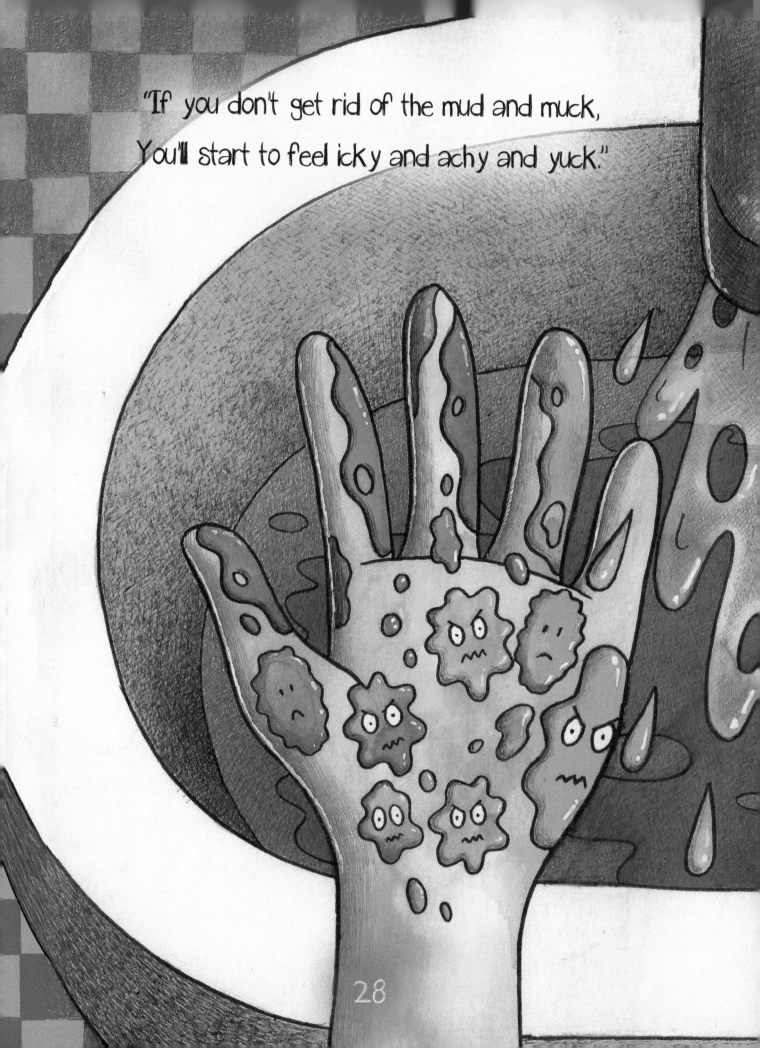

"If you don't get rid of the mud and muck,
You'll start to feel icky and achy and yuck."

28

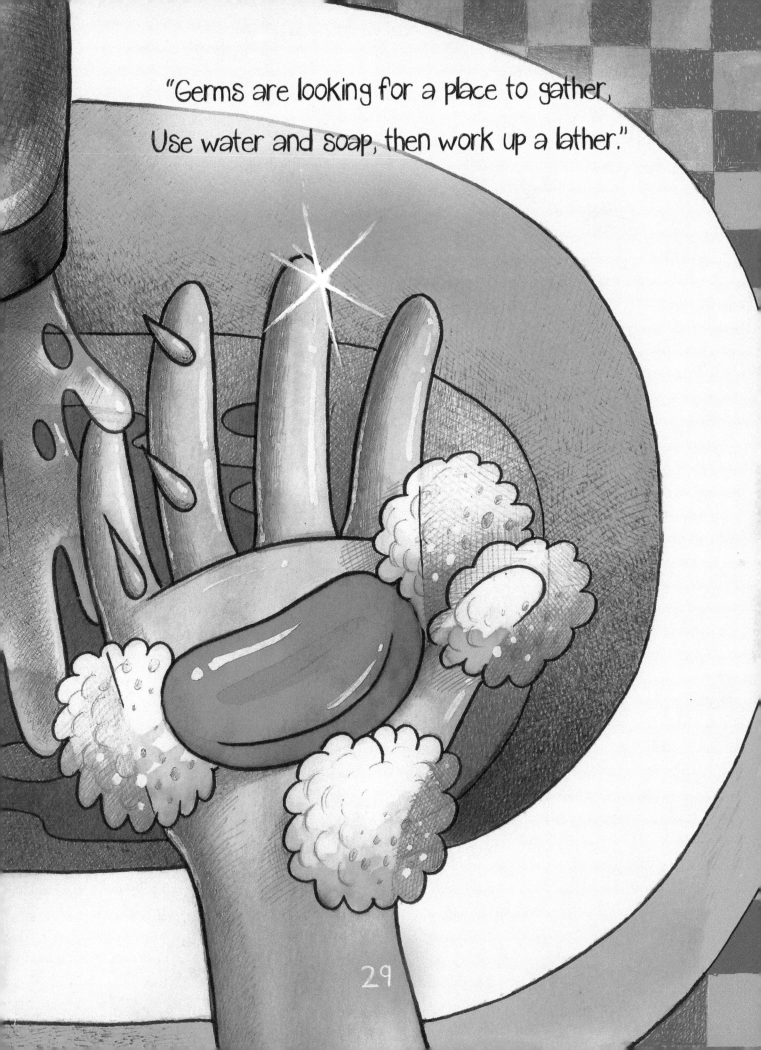

"Germs are looking for a place to gather,
Use water and soap, then work up a lather."

29

"There's no need to hurry, just take your time.
Soon you'll get rid of the filth and grime."

30

When the visit was over, Mom promised a treat.

Ice cream with sprinkles – Marcy's favorite sweet.

The next several days, Marcy took it easy.
When Saturday came, she was no longer sneezy.

She could not wait to get back outside,
Play rough and get dirty under the big blue sky.

33

But one thing had changed about Marcy McMann,
She always made sure to wash her hands!

35

Alison T Broderick wrote her debut book, "Samuel Stanley Scotty Snight," when she was 17 years old. A senior in high school, she was given an English assignment to create a poem based on the writings of award-winning author Shel Silverstein. Twenty-one years later, in December 2017, the book was published. "Marcy Mabel Mollie McMann" is the second book in her Healthy Habits Series. She lives in Marietta, Georgia, with her husband, two boys and Golden Retriever, Duke.

Visit www.AlisonTBroderick.com for more information.

Mina Anguelova, illustrator, was born in Sofia, Bulgaria. She moved to Portugal at the age of 4 years old. Mina has had many art exhibitions, one that stands out was her solo exhibition "Suspense" at the Monumental Art Gallery in Lisbon in 2011. As an animator and illustrator, Mina has taken part in the creation of many children's books and short movies.

Connect with Mina on Facebook at www.facebook.com/Minanguelova

Willow Moon Publishing

Wind and Water: A Love Story
The Little Dragon Flies in the Sun
Nobody Reads Haiku
Granny Kat's The Frog Prince (play adaptation)
Granny Kat's Sleeping Beauty (play adaptation)
S.H Levan's Cookbook: Recipes from Victorian Lancaster County
Samuel Stanley Scotty Snight
Make a Wish on a Fish
The Itch of Gloria Fitch: a play
Sweet Treats Book of Cupcakes: A Love You a Brunch Cookbook
Pepper, Ms. Pepperoni, Finds Someone to Love
On Halloween
Dancing Fea

https://willow-moon-publishing.com

Alison T Broderick's
The Healthy Habits Book Series

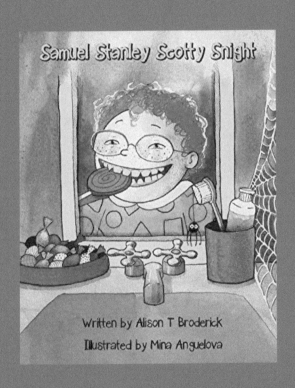

Book 3
Coming Soon

CPSIA information can be obtained
at www.ICGtesting.com
Printed in the USA
LVHW072149301118
598841LV00021B/443/P